CITY OF PLEASURE

CONNOR WHITELEY

No part of this book may be reproduced in any form or by any electronic or mechanical means. Including information storage, and retrieval systems, without written permission from the author except for the use of brief quotations in a book review.

This book is NOT legal, professional, medical, financial or any type of official advice.

Any questions about the book, rights licensing, or to contact the author, please email connorwhiteley@connorwhiteley.net

Copyright © 2022 CONNOR WHITELEY

All rights reserved.

DEDICATION
Thank you to all my readers without you I couldn't do what I love.

CHAPTER 1

Sitting on a wonderfully soft metal chair on a stone balcony that looked out over the City of Martyrs, even I have to admit this is actually a rather beautiful morning.

Normally I never ever would have considered a morning beautiful, bad or something, because after years of being a female assassin, life was just... well life. There wasn't anything good or bad about it, it was just something lived and enjoyed along the way towards my own inevitable death.

As I stared out over the City with miles upon miles of little white houses, thousands of lit candles burning and the amazing glassy ocean on the horizon, I knew being here was starting to benefit me. For the first time in my life, I felt whole, loving and I was really enjoying life.

From the table I picked up my large mug of coffee that filled the air with amazing hints of bitter coffee, hazelnuts and almonds. But when I took a warm sip of it, I wanted to gag at my entire mouth burnt of the strong almond syrup that people in the City used.

I have no idea why these people don't like to drink their coffee normally, but every single person here has to pour a liberal amount of almond syrup in their coffee. Apparently it's just part of the culture here, yet it's a part I would happily stamp out. I just needed to remember to ask for coffee without syrup in the future.

The sounds of people laughing, talking and joking about made a sense of calm wash over me as that was the reason I was still here. After me and the Rebellion freed the City of Martyrs a month ago everyone had been constantly having fun and enjoying their freedom.

Of course I had tried to enjoy this month of peace but I had pulled my weight too. For I knew my idiot of a father, the Overlord who ruled the Kingdom cruelly, would send an army to invade and retake the City after a while.

That and my favourite supernatural demons would return at some point too, surprisingly enough I was actually looking forward to fighting those three supernatural Hunters again. I wanted to beat them, but even I doubted I could.

The sound of someone walking up behind me made me smile as I knew exactly who it was. It was the real reason I was still here and I hadn't travelled the Kingdom to do some more killing, my beautiful

Coleman with his amazing fit body, wonderful hair and those dark emerald eyes pulled out a chair to sit next to me.

Of course dating the leader of the Rebellion had its advantages and disadvantages, but being an assassin and separate from the rest of the Rebellion meant I didn't get bullied, picked on or accused of manipulating Coleman for my father.

The last person to accuse me of that lie had choked on his own blood.

For a few precious moments we just sat in silence, stared out over the City and admired our handy work. But I knew Coleman was here on official business, he knew not to disturb me (regardless of how handsome he was) during my morning coffee break.

Loosening my long black cloak and hood, I turned to him and blew him a kiss. It was still hard to imagine I had almost died without telling him how I felt but here we were together, a couple and the fate of the Kingdom rested on our shoulders.

And now we were together, the idea of losing Coleman was even harder for me to bear.

"You look beautiful this morning," Coleman said.

I was immediately suspicious.

"Not so bad yourself but why you here?" I asked.

He smiled. "Because I got an intelligence report,"

Bless him, as much as I love Coleman, what he classes as an intelligence report is simply a few men running away from the City, scouting the local area and reporting what they thought they saw to him. Some of it was lies, some of it was useful, most of it was useless.

I took another sip of my coffee to stop myself smiling.

"There are ten thousand Overlord Soldiers heading our way,"

I spat out my coffee. "What! How far away?"

"Two days march away. They'll be here no matter what and they seek to kill us all,"

Go figure! I always believed the Overlord's soldiers wanted a tea party with us.

I put my coffee down on the table. "Can the City hold?"

Coleman shrugged.

"Come on Coleman, I thought the Ruler Lord Castellan Richard was organising the defence,"

Coleman gestured if he could have some of my coffee. I shook my head.

"Fine, Lord Richard is busy. He oversaw most of the defence building but we left the final stage to Dragnist and Abbic,"

Don't get me wrong I love those two senior Rebels, they're great fighters and I love them to death. But I would not put them in charge of something that would decide the fate of hundreds of thousands and possibly the entire Kingdom.

"I see." I said. "What about a sea invasion?"

Coleman leant closer to me, as if there was a

chance of getting overheard on a completely silent balcony.

"Three ships have disappeared in the past few days. There's a chance the Overlord has sent an armada,"

This was getting serious. I had watched the defence plans get written up and build, I had ever suggested a few improvements from my decades of being an assassin. We had all focused on a massive wall that protected the City from an inland army.

We never considered a sea-based army to attack.

"So we're going to be facing an attack on two fronts," I said.

Coleman was silent.

"What?" I asked.

Coleman went to grab my hand but I gestured him to just drink my coffee.

"It turns out there was a spy for the Overlord and he knows about the temple under the City,"

Just great!

When we liberated the City from the Overlord's control I had the wonderful experience of being trapped, imprisoned and almost dying in a massive temple underneath the City. But since that delightful experience, I had found two other entrances to the Temple from beyond the City limits. And of course, to make matters even worse I had discovered that these entrances were countless.

Meaning it was damn well impossible to seal them all up.

"Please tell me you ordered for all the known entrances to be sealed," I said firmly.

"Yes, and all the known entrances into the City have been sealed. The soldiers will be able to get into the temple but not into the City,"

I blew him a kiss.

It turned out he wasn't as useless at preparing for a siege as I thought but none of this was good in the slightest. We were all going to be attacked without a proper army and without reinforcements.

Unless I changed that.

"How long do you think you peeps you hold out for?" I asked.

"Lord Castellan has good tactics, we have the Rebels and new recruits. Maybe a two days,"

Wow I loved Coleman but surviving a siege for two days was both impressive, and a tat pathetic considering I had been fighting full blown invasions for decades.

I stood up and gently rubbed his shoulder. "I need you to take control here, be at Richard's side and make sure he doesn't do anything stupid,"

Coleman just looked at me.

"Cole, you have experience in surviving sieges. You kept the Rebellion alive long enough for me to do my part, I need you to do it again,"

Coleman stood up and wrapped his wonderfully strong arms around me. "What are you going to do?"

"I... I'm going to find us allies and I know where to start but you aren't coming,"

Coleman looked to the ground as he knew exactly where I was heading. The City of Pleasure was one of the Overlord's strongholds where unless you were rich, powerful and noble, you were born into slavery and once you reached the age of 18 you were used as a sex toy for the rich.

It was where my beautiful Coleman had been held for so long before he was rescued and now I had to go there, get his revenge but most importantly find us allies.

"You know who to find?" Coleman asked, not looking me in the eye.

"Yea, there are a few Lords there that hate the Overlord. They have their own armies and I think I can get them to help us,"

Coleman looked at me and kissed me. I savoured those amazingly soft lips.

"Please don't get caught. Please don't become one of the slaves. I… I couldn't live with myself if-"

I kissed him again. "I'll be fine and I'll be back for you. I promise,"

Coleman's eyes turn wet and I knew exactly why. This wasn't a good place to go to especially as a woman and if I got caught then my life would be over, and the fate of the Kingdom would die too.

But most importantly, if I got caught then my beautiful, sexy Coleman would die.

And I couldn't allow that.

CHAPTER 2

Commander Coleman sat on a hard wooden chair around a grand oak table surrounded by tall men and women that were supposedly meant to be commanders, captains and generals.

Coleman had never met any of them before and he would have liked to believe some of them had combat experience and knew what it was like to fight against the Overlord. But that was beyond a joke now as he watched their elegant posh movements and he knew that they were all Richard's friends. Friends that had no idea what it was like to see your friends die on the battlefield.

The sound of their posh snobby laughter, talking about the weather and latest fashion and even their light breathing was starting to get Coleman angry. He had never minded the posh except when they started to abuse him as a child in the City of Pleasure.

But Coleman needed, wanted them to take this seriously. The entire City was about to be attacked on three fronts by the Overlord and the Overlord was not going to send amateurs here. The Overlord would want to send a clear message to any person who even considered for a second about joining the Rebellion.

Rebelling against him had consequences.

The idea of the Assassin running off to the City of Pleasure made Coleman's stomach twist, churn and tighten as he couldn't handle facing his childhood again. That City was full of predators, monsters and pure evil that no one should ever see.

But the Assassin was doing the right thing, she would find the support and get them to come, Coleman just hoped it would be in time to save himself.

Because these posh elegant faces that clearly had never seen real work or labour belonged to the people who Coleman doubted would ever save anyone but themselves.

The smell of their earthy, flowery and chemically perfumes assaulted Coleman's senses as he stood a tall man in shiny silver armour walk in and sat next to him at the head of the table.

Everyone fell silent as they looked upon the Lord Castellan Richard, Coleman still couldn't believe the amazing sights he had seen in the past month because of Richard's power. Richard had created armour from air, food from rock and water from wine.

And many more amazing things.

Coleman just hoped Richard was a good leader under the threat of annihilation.

Richard clicked his fingers and blue lightning shot across the room and everyone focused on him.

"Commander Coleman wishes to update us on the situation," Richard said.

Coleman's eyes widened at the unexpectedness of it. He had expected to be ignored throughout the entire thing.

"Thank you my Lord Castellan," Coleman said, looking at the other people. "The situation is dire,"

None of them seemed to be interested.

"Unless we act we will be slaughtered by the sea, underneath and land armies that are converging on our position. There are tens of thousands of soldiers coming here,"

The others were starting to look a bit more interested.

"We need to formulate a plan. Conscript all able-bodied men and women into the army. We need to fight, build our defences and ensure we can survive,"

One man stood up. Coleman hated his long blue silk robes and golden teeth.

"Why bother? If these so-called tens of thousands are coming here, we will die. We should spend our final days doing what we love and allow the Overlord to kill us,"

Coleman shot up. "No! There is one hope we have,"

The golden teeth man mockingly threw his arms up in the air.

"Oh yes, your girlfriend. Isn't she Overlord's

daughter?"

Everyone gasped.

Coleman hadn't been expecting that attack. He didn't even know how this man knew about the beautiful Assassin's past.

"Just admit it, Commander. The Assassin has gone off, you're safe. Is she threatening to kill you? Is that why you are creating these stories in some attempt to weaken ourselves?"

Coleman had no idea what to say to something like that, the Assassin hated her father, she was going to kill him that was a fact, and now Coleman was really starting to understand why she hated the politics of leadership so much.

"She is loyal to me. She will kill the Overlord and she has left to help us," Coleman said.

The Golden Teeth man smiled. "Where is she going?"

Coleman looked at Richard and he was frowning and gesturing him to tell everyone.

"Fine, she is going to head to the City of Pleasure,"

The golden teeth man started clapping. The air around him started to buzz.

"Thank you stupid Rebels, that is exactly what my Master wished to know,"

Coleman whipped out his sword.

Throwing it at the man.

The man disappeared in a puff of smoke.

Coleman just looked at Richard. "I presume he

was one of yours. And now I fear he has just teleported off to the Overlord and told him exactly where his... prey will be,"

Richard frowned.

"And on top of that, he now knows about our last-ditch attempt to ensure our survival,"

CHAPTER 3
49 Hours Until the Rebellion Falls

As I passed under the massive iron gates into the City of Pleasure I completely understand why it gets its name. All around me as I rode in on my horse were so-called beautiful women walking all over the muddy ground flirting and throwing themselves at whoever passed through the gate.

There was another woman on horseback in front of me, clearly a stuck-up noblewoman, and her horse was carefully guided by guards over to a group of young (and very attractive) young men. They must have only have been twenty or so, but they were attractive I'll give them that.

The air stunk of hormones, sweat and damp as I forced my horse to travel through the crowd of young women, guards and young men. I was hoping beyond hope that with my long black cloak and hood I would be mistaken for one of the Overlord's covert agents and allowed to pass without having to hire a young man.

But I feared I was sadly mistaken.

As I looked past all the young women that were trying to flirt with me, touch my legs and ask about my business, I stared at the massive spires of the City of Pleasure.

From what little I actually knew about the City, I saw there were thousands of little wooden houses where the slaves were chained and lived. Then there were the massive iron spires where the most precious slaves were kept for the on-demand use by their masters.

And that was what I was interested in. I once ran into (well my sword did) one of these Masters and he ever so kindly explained how these ten Masters ruled over the City in the Overlord's name and every so often they sent beautiful young women to the capital for the Overlord to use.

If I had told Coleman that little detail, or at least reminded him, then he never would have let me come, because there's a chance someone here knew about my mother. She was apparently the Overlord's true love then he slipped into madness, tyranny and had sex with hundreds of women in order to create my half-brothers and sisters.

I wasn't even sure I completely understood it all yet, but I was hoping that this City (or sex prison) would give me some answers.

Yet I had to go to these spires.

"You there,"

I rolled my eyes as a tall rather young and handsome guard in their horrible black armour walked up to my horse. I was interested in how he was looking at me because he clearly had no idea what to do with me.

He probably knew I was strange with my long black cloak and hood, and I clearly wasn't a Lord, Lady or an obvious member of the Overlord's inner circle. So unlike most people he didn't know where to send me.

"What is your business here?" he asked.

I playfully stroked his cheeks. "Well darling, I do what one must in the City of Pleasure. Now darling can I hire you?"

As the guard's cheeks lit up like a fire, I forced myself not to laugh. Now he really didn't know what to do with me.

"If you want young men, my Lady, I suggest you go to Lord Master Gillman. He has a plentiful supply of young men for your entertainment. There is even a rumour that he enhances his boys,"

"Thank you darling, I hope we meet again," I said, blowing him a kiss.

"Wait Miss, you need this," the guard said fluttered as he passed me a sheet of parchment saying I was allowed into the City.

That's something else I loved about this job, sure sometimes you need to sneak about, kill a bunch of people and do mass damage. But other times you simply need to let laypeople do their jobs and they make your job ten times easier.

I stroked my horse and we started to move through the crowd until a bunch of young women started dancing in front of me.

I knew these dances only lasted a minute or two or three but behind me I heard a number of horses stop and talk to the guards.

"My Lord Hunters," the guard said.

Shit! Shit! Shit!

I couldn't have those supernatural Hunters here yet. I didn't think they could find me so easily. I didn't even know they would be normal, I thought the guard would have fled at the sight of them.

"There is an assassin here. A best of the Rebellion. We must hunt her. Hunt her soul. Have you seen her? One of the Rebels told us she was here before we killed him,"

Damn it!

Now the Overlord and Hunters clearly knew exactly what I was up to. There must have been some kind of spy in the Rebellion and my beautiful but far too trusting boyfriend, clearly told others about my mission.

I hated it when this happened.

Logically it might have been an idea to run off, escape and try and kill the Hunters, but I was hoping they weren't going to see me.

"My Lords, what does she look like? We must stop her,"

I didn't need to look behind me to know the

Hunters were looking and breathing in my direction.

"We agree. Do you know where she is?"

"No, my Lords,"

I tensed as I heard this neck snap.

"He lies. She is within the City. He saw her. He loved her. She… is there!"

I jumped off my horse.

The Hunters screamed.

My ears bleed.

I ran deeper into the City.

I had to survive.

CHAPTER 4
48 Hours Until The Rebellion Falls

Commander Coleman wanted to destroy the entire damn Overlord army as he stood on top of the massive yellow stone wall that was meant to be their bulwark against the attack.

For the past two days everyone in the City had been helping to finish the wall, it completely ringed around the land facing parts of the City making it impossible for the Overlord's army to go around the wall.

The enemy would have to go through the wall.

That was meant to give Coleman some comfort yet it really didn't. He wanted a sure-fire way to keep the enemy out of the City but after watching people finish off the wall for the past few days, he wasn't sure if the wall couldn't withstand an assault.

It might last twelve hours but much of the wall hadn't been made out of granite and Coleman hated that. He had commanded Richard to build the wall out of granite but that was never going to happen.

Coleman understood that partly, granite did take a while to mine, cut and lift into place but it was just infuriating that the wall wasn't going to be as strong as it needed to be.

The entire wall was a beautiful marvel of engineering and determination on the people's part to stay alive, Coleman couldn't have been prouder of these people.

Especially with the grand solid granite towers that ran along the wall like imposing giants.

The sound of marching made from the distance and Coleman knew this was just the calm before the storm. All around him stood rows upon rows of archers armed with bows and crossbows. As soon as the enemy were in range they needed to fire, the archers had to buy the rest of them as much time as possible.

But Coleman still couldn't forgive himself for telling that enemy spy the plans, he didn't want to imagine he had put his stunning Assassin with that amazing body, hair and cloak in danger. But he knew he had.

He couldn't afford to make that mistake again. He just hoped this top secret backup plan he had made with Abbic, his closest friend, was going to work. Coleman hoped that if nothing else, Abbic could get the chemicals, potions and powder she found in a vault to work once more. Coleman didn't have high hopes for Abbic's chemical abilities.

The smell of horrid rotten meat filled the air as pink lumps were flying through the air towards the City. Thankfully the lumps of meat hit the wall and bounced off outside the City.

If they were as disease filled as Coleman feared he didn't want anyone touching them, he made a mental note to inform everyone of disease protocols. But that meant something else too, the enemy had catapults or something that could throw projectiles grand distances. And it was only a matter of time before those lumps of meat became something far more destructive.

Lumps of rock.

Coleman felt his stomach tighten as he imagined all the bloodshed, death and destruction this attack was going to bring down on the City. It wasn't fair, it wasn't right, it wasn't just.

It was life.

Ever since his father had gifted him control of the Rebellion, Coleman knew one day he would fight not for the survival of the Rebellion, he had done that before, but for the very survival of the idea of freedom.

If the City of Martyrs fell then it would send a shockwave through the entire Kingdom telling them that no one ever sides with the Rebellion and gets to live.

Coleman felt his skin turn white as he realised that this wasn't a mission for the enemy to retake the City. This was a mission to annihilate them all.

The enemy was never going to allow anyone to survive. The Overlord probably wanted to carry their bodies through each of the other Cities as proof of his supremacy.

Coleman wasn't going to allow that. He was going to deny the enemy that message and he was going to send out a message about the Overlord's weakness throughout the Kingdom, even if it meant sacrificing himself in the process.

Actually that wasn't a bad idea. Coleman started walking along the massive wall, passing each of the archers that were preparing themselves and went over to one of the towers in the wall.

Coleman loved this tower the best because unlike the others that had massive braziers, with their towering piles of wood inside an immense metal pan, this tower had crates upon crates of birds.

The three women who stood there aiming their crossbows at the incoming enemy were definitely Rebels at heart. Their posture was perfect, their rage was controlled and these three wanted to slaughter the enemy. That bought Coleman some level of peace at least.

"Excuse me?" Coleman said.

The three women turned and spoke as one.

"Commander Coleman," they greeted.

"I need you all to help me with a massive favour,"

They nodded.

"Do you have a pack of parchment, ink and

string up here?" Coleman asked.

The women looked at each other like Coleman was clueless before they bend down and picked up the supplies.

"Great. We need to send out a message to all settlements in the Kingdom,"

"What?" the women asked.

"I know there are a lot of settlements but the birds can fly to them all. I just need a simple message sent,"

The women looked at each other and nodded.

"Fine, what do ya wanted Commander?"

"We need to tell every single settlement that the City of Martyrs stands with everyone,"

The women were about to start writing but they stopped.

"Is that it?" they asked.

It was really creepy now how they spoke.

Coleman looked out over the wall and saw the ten thousand soldiers and their catapults marching at full speed towards them.

The Catapults fired.

The battle had started.

"It's all we have time for,"

CHAPTER 5

47.5 Hours Until The Rebellion Falls

After I barely managed to escape those idiot Hunters, I sold my horse to some young men and hoped that they would escape in time and get away from this sex-focused hell hole.

As I knelt on a cold wooden roof that was attached to one of the endless wooden houses that homed the sex slaves for the Masters of the City of Pleasure, I made sure my long black cloak and hood were tightly covering me as I stared down on the street below. I was a little concerned at first that I might be seen but the more time passed, the more I was starting to understand how the City worked.

The entire City was basically built upon the idea that no Master, noble or anyone with any power walked the streets, and those that did only went onto these streets for one purpose.

To get beautiful fit young men and women to bring back to their spires so they would do the deed and then dump them back out onto the streets. And judging by the conversations I've overheard if the sex slave does a good job at the pleasing the Master (which I learnt was the title for both men and women with powers here) then the slave might get a bowl of food, or even a bit of money.

Apparently the slaves could buy their freedom but as an assassin who's been killing for a good two decades, I know that was an absolute lie. People born in the City of Pleasure would only ever be used for one purpose- sex slavery.

It was disgusting, outrageous and it made my blood boil. This was stupid on so many levels and the Overlord would know my feelings on the topic sooner or later.

The smell of hormones, sweat and perfume filled the air to create a horrid concoction that I really didn't want to smell anymore so I started to move across the rooftops. Jumping from one wooden house to another.

Well, I say jump, it's more like hop because all these houses are so close together if there was a fire, it would only take a few minutes for the entire street to be alight.

As I hopped across the rooftops, I focused on the massive iron spires that rose high into the sky in the distance. The sheer scale of the City of Pleasure was starting to strike me as it must have taken years if not decades to build all these miles upon miles of wooden houses only for the iron Spires to be perfectly centred in the middle.

I suppose in a way the spires had to be in the dead centre of the City, because those poor sex Masters wouldn't want to have to go too far, or further than another Master, to get their prey.

As much as I wanted, needed to free these people and kill all their Masters, I needed to remind myself that I wasn't here for them directly. I was here to find the Lords that hated the Overlord, had their private armies and were willing to help the Rebellion against the Overlord's invasion.

My stomach tightened as I imagined what was happening in the City of Martyrs. I didn't even know if the City still stood, I didn't know if my beautiful Coleman was alive and I most certainly didn't know if our 48 hour window was still that long.

The sound of whispering followed by deadly silence filled the street below me as I knew the Hunters were riding along looking for me.

This wasn't good. I didn't need them here, not right now. I needed them to leave me alone, carry out my work but after I killed the woman who apparently birthed them on my last mission, I highly doubt they were ever going to leave me alone.

"Have you seen her?" one of the Hunters asked a young woman on the street.

I instantly stopped moving and knelt closer to the edge of the rooftop. Of course it was an amateur mistake but I couldn't leave unless I knew there was nothing, absolutely nothing I could have done to save the young woman.

Then one by one each of the young men and women in the street started to look around. Some were even looking up and I realised something in that moment, all these sex slaves were interested in keeping each other safe. They didn't want to live like this, they wanted to be safe, free and protected.

That's something I could definitely use.

Young men and women started to jump out the way as a horse-drawn carriage threatened towards the Hunters.

But they didn't seem concerned, threatened or nothing.

They just stood there in their long shadowy cloaks and faces made from shadow stared coldly at the carriage.

After a few seconds, the carriage stopped and out stepped a short man wearing long golden robes that were covered in jewels, fine silks and even packs of food were hanging from his waist.

And as the man looked at each of the young people in the street, he didn't look menacing, happy or like a predator, he actually looked sad for each of them.

After killing for as long as I have, I like to believe I can read people well and this man was far from the evil, predator that this City bred into the rich and powerful. I truly believe if this man could, he would happily take over the City and free everyone.

That was definitely something to take note of.

"Leave this City!" the man shouted.

The Hunters stared at him. "We are the Hunters. We never leave. Our prey is here. We-"

"Are leaving. I know the Overlord has you under this control. But if you leave I can promise you your day of freedom will get closer,"

Now that was interesting.

Even the Hunters seemed to look at each other and they even took a step away from the man.

"The Day of Freedom is a myth. Only the Overlord can free us. He will never free us,"

The man smiled. "I promise you if you live the Assassin and me live in peace for six hours. Your freedom day will get closer,"

The Hunters hissed, shrieked and moaned with each other. It was awful to listen to, it sounded like dying animals but they were clearly considering the offer.

What I wanted to know was how the man knew I was here in the first place, and it wouldn't have surprised me if he knew I was in earshot.

"Six hours then we execute the Overlord's command," the Hunters said as one as they all disappeared in the wind.

I jumped off the rooftop and landed on the top of the carriage.

The man turned around and smiled. He was actually glad to see me.

"Assassin, it has been a long time. I have waited for this day for even longer. Come, we have much to discuss," the man said.

The only problem was, I had never met this man before in my life and he clearly knew about me.

And that unnerved me more than I wanted to admit.

CHAPTER 6
47.5 Hours Until The Rebellion Falls

Commander Coleman stared with utter horror as the disgraceful Overlord's army in their ten thousand marched towards the Wall. Coleman had never imagined he would have to face this many foes, he never wanted to.

But now the entire fate of the City of Martyrs rested on his shoulders.

Coleman had to lead the Wall's defence, he had to marshal the strength of the brave men and women that stood by him properly, he had to be brave. Because he knew with all certainty that if he failed then the Rebellion would be slaughtered and Coleman could never allow that to happen.

All around Coleman on the massive Wall stood archers aiming their bows and on his command they would fire, unleashing extreme amounts of fury at the Overlord.

The sounds of massive chunks of rock smashing

in front of the wall filled the air as the enemy's catapult tried to stop it. As much as Coleman wanted to believe the Wall would always stand, that was a lie and he knew it.

Sooner or later that catapult would be within range and the Wall's time would be limited. If that was Coleman's only problem then he might not have cared, but considering there could be an army coming up under the City would the underground Temple and a sea invasion.

Coleman wasn't impressed.

Then he noticed every single man and woman on the Wall was staring at Coleman waiting for his command.

Coleman took out his swords and took a deep breath of the sandy air. This was where history would define Coleman, so he wanted to make it memorable.

"Fire!" Coleman shouted.

As soon as Coleman gave the order hundreds of arrows fired into the air, screaming towards the Overlord's men and then it had truly begun.

The battle for the City of Martyrs had started and now Coleman's entire fate rested in the hands of his beautiful Assassin.

The arrows slaughtered the enemy.

They screamed.

The Archers fired again.

More arrows flew through the air.

Hammering into the enemy.

Peppering bodies with holes.

The catapults were getting closer.

The Archers fired again.

More enemies screamed in agony.

Coleman pointed his sword at the Catapults.

He could see them now.

The enemy was loading rocks into them.

They were flaming rocks.

The enemy was turning them.

Coleman's stomach tightened.

The Catapults fired.

Flaming rocks screamed towards Coleman.

They were dropping.

Dropping fast.

Coleman didn't order anyone to move.

The rocks smashed into the base of the wall.

Coleman felt a vibration.

No damage done.

The Wall stood.

Coleman ordered the Archers again.

They fired.

The enemy stopped marching. They stood still. They were waiting.

Coleman went to say something.

The enemy charged.

They broke formation.

The archers fired.

Arrows flew high into the sky.

They slammed into the enemy.

The enemy kept moving.

They were quick.

They were getting closer to the Wall.

Closer and closer.

Coleman needed to do something.

He had to act.

The catapults were moving fast.

Coleman focused on them. The enemy were pushing them. The Catapults were within range.

The catapults fired.

Flaming rocks flew towards the Wall.

Coleman shouted a warning.

But by the time the warning left his mouth it was too late. The massive flaming rocks slammed into the Wall.

Coleman grabbed onto anything as he struggled to remain standing. Shockwave after shockwave ripped through his body.

People were thrown off the wall. Slamming onto the ground below.

Coleman forced himself up. The Archers were in chaos. The enemy was almost at the Wall. All ten thousand of them.

The Catapults were getting nearer and nearer. Soon they'll be able to attack the City. Burning it to the ground.

Coleman ordered the archers to never stop firing. And he started to walk away. He had to get rid of those catapults even if it killed him.

Screams echoed all around the City of Martyrs. Coleman looked over the edge of the Wall inside the City.

His eyes widened as he saw black armoured soldiers walking around his City killing his people and defenders.

He was right. The Overlord's army had come through the underground temple. They were now being attacked on two fronts. This wasn't good. Coleman needed help. He needed to fight.

He needed his Assassin.

Coleman grabbed onto the Wall as more flaming rocks slammed into it.

Time was running out fast and scared Coleman more than anything!

CHAPTER 7
47 Hours Until The Rebellion Falls

Well I have to say that carriage ride through the City was awful, simply awful. My long black cloak and hood kept getting caught on the fixtures, and I have never experienced such a slow and bumpy ride through streets. Yes I know there were tons of people, young beautiful men and women, but they need to learn to get out of the way.

I am trying to save them after all!

Anyway I am more than happy that the carriage is over, as I went into a small office filled with walls lined with bookcases, a small brown desk in the centre with no chairs. But I did have a soft spot for the massive golden bed tucked away in the corner.

Now I will not have sex with this man whatsoever, I only have sex with my Coleman with those amazing dark emerald eyes, but I can appreciate the man's preparedness at least.

The air smelt of utter awful hints of jasmine, rose

and chocolate that was clearly designed to bring young women (or men) back here and seduce completely into the man's grip.

But what I did find strange about it all was the office (and this was presumably his living quarters too) was on the lowest level of the Spires. I would have thought that a man who acted like this would be more powerful, and my opinion it was the more powerful people lived at the top of the spires.

Then of course I remembered that I was in the City of Pleasure and nothing was ever it seemed. And in all honesty, the most powerful people probably lived at the bottom so they didn't need to carry their slaves too far and waste precious time where they could be shagging them instead of carrying them.

The sound of the wooden door closing made me really focus on the man with his long expensive robes, jewels and fine silks. All the food packs that hung from his waist were now gone as he threw them out of the window as we rode.

I even threw the money I got from selling my horse out too. I had to give these poor slaves something to make their lives better.

The man made sure the door was locked and went over to his desk sat on it. Then it twigged how clear the desk was and I instantly knew that was the desk was a nice hard surface for a rougher time for the slaves.

"Tell me why I shouldn't kill you now for using sex slaves?" I asked.

The man cocked his head. "Because Assassin you know I don't support their slavery and look at my desk. Is there a drop of sweat, cum or blood on it?"

I didn't need to check it to know he was telling the truth.

"Fine, what is the Day of Freedom to the Hunters?" I asked, going over to inspect the bed.

"The Day of Freedom is a prophecy that spells the end of the Overlord's enslavement of the Hunters and there are two ways to free the Hunters,"

"And if we free the Hunters they will leave the Kingdom?"

"Assassin, they will leave this world forever,"

I went over to him. "How do we free them?"

Of course I could have been a bit eager but I didn't want to spend the rest of my life running, fighting and risking Coleman's life with the Hunters' threat.

"I have a map in my possession that details the location of an Oath rod that if broken can free the Hunters,"

It was interesting enough that there was a map for an Oath Rod. They were funny creations because they were only a long rod with detailed carvings of ivory, but when two (or more) people held them and made an oath. It made the oath unbreakable.

Yet if the oath rod was damaged enough or outright destroyed then the oath never existed in magical law. And I fully believe the Hunters wanted that more than anything else in the world.

"Give me the map," I said firmly.

The man opened his desk and took out a tiny

piece of parchment.

"The City of Martyrs stands with everyone," he said.

I instantly knew it was from Coleman and my stomach tightened more and more as I feared the worse. I forced myself to stay put and not run off towards the City to save him.

The man smiled. "I am Lord Gillman. I met you once when you were a baby and your mother was shipped off to the Capital. I was her best friend and I… I really tried to keep her hidden, but she loved the Overlord too much,"

I bit my lip.

"I know you want me to tell you everything and I promise you I will. I will give you the map, your history, everything. Just help me please," Gillman said.

Normally I might have been cocky, arrogant or just and horrible person but today I wanted to be kind. I took Gillman's hand and rubbed it gently.

"What do I need to do?" I asked.

He beamed at that. "As you can probably guess, the powerful, most richest members of the City live on the bottom of the Spires,"

I knew it!"

"My money, possession and supplies are safely stored away, so I want you to do what you're best at,"

I just looked at him.

"News of your destroying the Grand Cathedral in the City of Martyrs reached me. Think you could destroy the Spires?" he asked.

I shook my head. "I could easily but the shockwave and damage caused by the four spires falling would kill more slaves than save,"

Gillman nodded. "Fine. I will arrange a meeting of the Masters and you will be there. Kill them all and I will gather you an army,"

I cocked my head at that. "But with the Masters' dead, the City would be free anyway right?"

"Oh Assassin, no. There are stories that the Masters bring certain slaves into the Spires not for their own pleasure but the pleasure of a True Master. They aren't stories,"

CHAPTER 8
46.5 Hours Until The Rebellion Falls

Coleman slashed the throat of another horrible black armoured soldier and as the corpse fell to the ground, covering the yellow cobblestones in deep red blood, he couldn't believe how bold and stupid the Overlord's soldiers were being.

It was bad enough they were attacking the City with Catapults that smashed flaming rocks into the Wall every few minutes but now they were infiltrating the City.

That was outrageous.

It wasn't a gentleman tactic, it wasn't honourable and it certainly wasn't going to help Coleman save his people. And to make matters worse, Coleman hadn't seen, hear and smelt any allies nearby for half an hour.

Coleman looked around at the little white houses that all stood around him like some judgemental parents who were going to tell him off for not doing his best. Coleman had to find allies, friends and anyone who was still alive.

Because that was his greatest fear, not only could he be the last man in the City standing with only those on the Wall left, but he could be the last man to be hunted down and slaughtered of by the Overlord's soldiers.

The sound of sword clashing and smashing and lashing in the distance made Coleman breathe a sigh of relief as at least he knew he wasn't alone. But if he didn't help, he didn't know how much that still rang true.

Coleman ran through the streets.

Passing white house after house. The cobblestone streets were wet with blood. Corpses littered the ground.

Coleman turned a corner.

Ten enemy soldiers stood there. Smashing down the door of a house. They were going to attack innocent people.

Coleman flew at them.

Slashing his sword.

Slicing into their armour.

Their armour shattered.

Breaking off.

Coleman didn't stop.

He kicked them.

Punched them.

Slashed.

Blood spattered up white walls.

Coleman rammed his sword into their chests.

The soldiers were too slow.

The door opened.

Rebels poured out.

Lashing the enemy's chest.

Blood poured out.

Screams echoed all around.

Coleman charged again.

His sword swinging madly.

Hacking the enemies to pieces.

With ten corpses hacked to multiple pieces lying at their feet, Coleman took a deep breath of the cold air that was filled with plenty of vapourised blood. He looked at the Rebels and nodded his thanks.

"Good job everyone," Coleman said, looking around for any more foes.

One of the Rebels, a wall woman with short hair, leather armour and two swords, stepped forward.

"Thank you ma Lord. We saw 'em coming out of the main sewage tunnels near the old Grand Cathedral,"

If Coleman wasn't focused on staying alive, he would have kissed her for that information. At last he knew exactly where the enemy were coming from. It made perfect sense, all the other known entrances were sealed and that sewage entrance was definitely not known about.

Coleman had to seal it now. But he had to give the Overlord's soldiers credit, he wouldn't want to crawl through thousands of litres of raw sewage just to kill some people.

"Thank you. With me," Coleman said, firmly.

Coleman and his newfound Rebels went to start running but twenty black armoured soldiers stood there pointing their crossbows at them.

Aiming at their chests.

A tall man wearing spiked armour walked to the front of his men and sneered at Coleman.

"I look forward to delivering your head to the Overlord," he said to Coleman.

Coleman pointed his sword at him. "That will never happen,"

"Fire!" the man shouted.

Crossbows fired.

The Rebels ducked.

Coleman was too slow.

The arrows screamed towards them.

An arrow ripped into Coleman's flesh.

Coleman hit the ground.

He hissed.

The enemy reloaded.

The Rebels charged.

Whipping out their swords.

They hacked the enemy to pieces.

Coleman heard something.

More soldiers were coming behind them.

Coleman forced himself up. He grabbed his sword. He went to swing it at them.

Another arrow rammed itself into his back.

Coleman collapsed to the ground.

He felt the blood oozing out of him. The Rebels

were surrounded. Both sets of soldiers got closer.

They were doomed.

White magical lightning shot through the air.

Turning the soldiers to ash.

Archers flooded the streets.

Slaughtering the soldiers.

Corpses slammed to the ground.

Coleman hissed. He forced himself up to see one of the few people he actually wanted to see at a time like this. Lord Castellan Richard swirled and twirled and whirled his magical energy at the enemy reducing them to ash.

As Richard's Archers secured the street, Richard marched over to Coleman and covered Coleman's face with his hands.

Coleman didn't like it at first but as he felt magical energy seep into his flesh and his wounds heal themselves, he started to learn to like it.

Richard took away his hand and Coleman nodded his thanks to him.

"These are dark times to travel alone Commander," Richard said.

"Agreed my Lord. We must go to the main sewage tunnels, the enemy are coming from there,"

Richard frowned. "My powers are needed at the Wall. But take my personal archers,"

The entire City shook as more flaming rocks slammed into the Wall. But to Coleman's utter horror massive chunks of stone fell off the Wall.

And now it had truly begun. The Wall's time was

running out as Coleman knew each and every hit would weaken it more and more and more until the Wall collapsed entirely.

Then ten thousand soldiers would swarm the City of Martyrs and kill everyone.

Coleman couldn't let that happen. He just didn't know how to stop it.

Yet.

CHAPTER 9
44 Hours Until the Rebellion Falls

When Lord Gillman said he was going to call a Meeting of the Masters, I was expecting something rather evil, posh and very, very condensing. I did not expect to be hiding in what could easily be mistaken for a sex shop.

With my long black cloak and hood tightly wrapped around me, I hung onto an extremely disturbing chandelier. Normally chandeliers are made from wonderful gold, jewels and silver.

Oh no, this one was made from gold mixed with blood, skulls with the candles sitting in the mouths and another one of my favourites, human hair was the only thing holding it all up.

Seriously!

I mean how stupid, perverse and just utter wrong can you yet. If I had actually come here today not knowing why I was going to kill all these Masters, I certainly knew why now.

As the smell of roasted meat, manly sweat and semen filled the air, I looked down onto the massive feast table below. Considering the slaves didn't get much food (they only got enough of the right food to keep their muscles big and their bodies slim), this must have a punch in the stomach to the slaves attending.

There were ten people (five women, five men) sitting at the table wearing long sexualised leather pants and tops. Each one held a leash for their slave in one hand and in the other they held a fine glass of red wine. But to only add to the disturbing nature of the meeting, on the table in front of them were what only be described as... sex instruments.

There were whips, chains, gags and plenty more things I had never seen or wanted to use in my life. I almost feel sorry for the slaves but that's when I realised they wanted to be here more than their Masters.

Of course, don't get me wrong, I could "understand" the possible thrill they might get from a group session. But clearly these slaves were not in the right mindset considering some of those so-called sex instruments, I could easily use to kill people.

So as harsh as it sounded, I was far from concerned if I killed a few slaves in the process. Especially as these slaves would probably come to the aid of their Masters.

A tall man in shiny leather stood up at the head of the table and raised his glass to everyone.

"Today we dine for the Glory of the True Master. May he give us as much as pleasure as we give him,"

Wow!

I had to kill these people now before I vowed never to have sex again!

I jumped down.

Landing on the table.

Whipping out my swords.

I swirled on the table.

Slashing four throats.

Their slaves jumped up.

Running at me.

I kicked them.

I slashed them.

I killed them.

The other Masters grabbed a weapon.

I kicked food at them.

Some food whacked them.

I flew over.

Ramming my swords into their chests.

Three more died that way.

A Master whipped me.

I spun around.

Jumping on her.

I snapped her neck.

Slaves pounced on me.

Punching me.

Smashing their fists into me.

Enough was enough.

I jumped into the air.

Spinning out.

Extending my swords.

My swords slit their throats.

Blood poured all over the food.

Three Masters left.

But as I stood up on the table to prepare to strike, I saw all three of them (Three women) were clapping at me. They were smiling, but it was an erotic smile. These women enjoyed the killing.

In fact, I'm sure all of them properly thought this was part of the Lord Gillman's plan at calling the meeting. They probably all got off on violence.

I threw my swords at them.

The swords skewered two of the women.

Now she was the only one left, the last woman in her dull leather suit looked so helpless and pathetic as the enjoyment drained from her face.

"You... you aren't friend, are you?" she asked.

I went over to her and ripped my swords out of her friends.

"You go... going to kill me?"

I looked at her undecided, I knew I was going to kill her but I at least could have given her a sense of false security.

"Where is the True Master?" I asked.

I wondered if she was going to orgasm at his name, but she looked like she was suppressing the urge well. (I really wanted to escape this place now!)

"He is everywhere. He will come for you now. He will come for Lord Gillman. As a Master Gillman has to give him his pleasure now,"

The hairs on my neck started to stand up as I felt like something was starting to dawn on me but I couldn't say it. It was on the tip of my tongue what she was hinting at.

"Does Lord Gillman know this?"

"Course not, the True Master loves us all. He only picks one Master to give him pleasure at any one time. He is old-fashioned that way,"

Now it dawned on me.

"Will the True Master kidnap Gillman?" I asked.

The woman cocked her head. "It will not be kidnapping. We all love the True Master. We-"

I snapped her neck.

Running off.

I had to find Gillman.

I couldn't let the True Master take my only hope of learning about myself and saving the man I loved.

CHAPTER 10
44 Hours Until the Rebellion Falls

Coleman peeked around a corner of a little white house to look at the massive entrance to the main sewage tunnels that not only connected the impressive sewage system to the underground Temple, but provided a perfect entrance into the City for the enemy.

Coleman hated everything about the entrance with its large black manhole cover that was big enough to throw cattle down there without a problem.

But the smell of poo, raw sewage and rotten flesh was immense. The idea was ridiculous that the Overlord's soldiers would willingly travel into the underground Temple and into the sewage network. Yet the Overlord's soldiers were stupid, persistent and loyal to a fault (literally) to their Overlord Master.

Coleman focused on the massive amount of rubble, chunks of stone and corpses that littered the area around the entrance to the sewage tunnels. His beautiful sexy Assassin had done amazingly on their last mission when she burned down the Cathedral.

But now the little square (or what remained of it) looked sad, dystopian and horrific without a complete building. Yet that was the cost of war with the Overlord.

The sound of something tapping against metal and metal moving made Coleman stare at the manhole cover as it moved and it was lifted up.

Revealing an endless stream of foul armoured soldiers pouring into the City like they owned the place. Coleman might be able to understand them if they had tried to be sneaky or at least careful about their infiltration. But that was the last thing they were doing.

These soldiers looked so confident, so assured, so arrogant that no one was going to notice if they slipped and killed a bunch of people who only wanted freedom. And that really pissed Coleman off.

He took out his swords and looked at his ten Rebels (more had sadly died on the way here) and the five personal archers that Richard had lent him. They were all ready with their weapons to storm over and slaughter the enemy.

They all nodded to Coleman.

Coleman whipped out his sword and charged.

Feet pounding into the cobblestone.

The soldiers turned.

Their eyes widened.

They were too slow.

Coleman jumped into the air.

Twirling his sword

Slashing their throats.

They screamed.

The Rebels stormed over.

Swinging their swords.

Hacking into the enemy.

Blood flooded the ground.

The enemy died.

More soldiers kept coming out.

Coleman kept fighting.

The Archers fired. Again and again.

Arrows screamed through the air. Ripping into the soldier's flesh.

Someone whacked him in the head.

Throwing him to the ground.

They picked him up by the throat.

They started crushing him.

Coleman looked at the muscular woman. She was twice the size of him.

Her muscles bulged.

She was going to kill him.

Coleman struggled. It was useless. His vision blurred.

Arrows shot into the woman's brain. It didn't help.

Rebels slashed at the woman's head.

The Rebels stabbed her muscles.

Cutting them away.

She dropped Coleman.

Coleman gasped for air.

More enemies came out.

Coleman picked up his sword.

He flew at them.

Their blades slashed.

Sparks flying.

They were stronger.

They merciless swung at Coleman.

There were too many.

The City shook again. More flaming rocks slammed into the Wall. More of it collapsed.

The air whistled.

The air turned warm.

Coleman kicked a soldier.

He looked up.

A flaming rock was hurling toward them.

Coleman ran.

The rock smashed into the square.

Creating a shockwave.

Creating a dust cloud.

Throwing Coleman forward.

He smashed into a little white house.

As Coleman kept coughing more and more as the dust invaded his lungs, he shook his hands around to try and clear the dust away. He was horrified to see the massive flaming rock was burning uncontrollably in the square.

But Coleman had to smile as he saw the smouldering corpses of the enemy soldiers lying there, and when he closed his eyes and truly focused, he could barely hear the screams of agony of the soldiers underground as the flames caught them.

And one of the most scary things about sewages was how flammable they were, all that sewage, rot and poo created more than enough methane to ignite and Coleman had little doubt it had already gone off.

In that moment he was extremely grateful for the thick stone walls of the sewage network, at least the methane explosion was contained.

Coleman looked around but it dawned on him that so few of the Rebels and Archers were standing. There was a group of three Rebels standing next to some flaming corpses and the two Archers were kneeling on the ground in front of some more.

A wave of discomfort washed over Coleman as he realised he might have succeeded in fighting off the soldiers, but he had failed at protecting the brave men and women that looked to him.

The entire City shook again as more flaming rocks smashed into the Wall and a massive whoosh echoed around the City as an immense chunk of the Wall collapsed. Creating a thick choking dust cloud.

As Coleman focused on the Wall, he was glad that the chunk that had collapsed was still too high for the ten thousand enemy soldiers to jump, walk or climb over.

But that would happen in only a matter of time.

Coleman had to destroy the Catapults. He had to buy his beautiful Assassin more time. He had to risk his life to save the City.

And he wouldn't have it any other way.

"Want to destroy some Catapults?" Coleman asked.

All the remaining Archers and Rebels went over to Coleman and to his surprise they smiled.

"Let's burn them to the ground," Coleman said.

CHAPTER 11
42 Hours Until the Rebellion Falls

This was ridiculous!

How dare these stupid Masters allow themselves to give pleasure, servitude and lives to this so-called True Master. When I found him I was going to gut him from head to stomach and legs. I was not kidding around here.

No one even thinks about threatening my only hope and gets to live.

But as I went into his office with the massive golden bed in the corner and the small desk, I realised someone had gotten here before me. And I was livered.

The desk was knocked off and the bed was completely dirty and unmade. Completely outrageous and stupid because I now had to find the True Master, but of course I do not know what he looks like. I then need to save Lord Gillman and I need him to give me his private army.

I went to go over to the small desk when I felt something wet under my feet. It was blood. I loosened my long black cloak and hood as I knelt down to inspect it.

The blood was in a large pool in front of me, it was fresh. I tasted it. Definitely human, had plenty of iron it so clearly from a man and there was a hint of vitality in it. So I was looking at the blood of a young man.

Then as I knelt on the ground, I noticed that a good amount of blood was starting to drip down onto the ground from the bed. So I went to it and lifted up the sheets. Revealing a corpse.

The young man's corpse was still warm to the touch, the man himself was probably 25 years old and had massive scars all over his body. Probably from his Masters (I was more than glad I had killed them now). But the killing blows looked weird.

There were two large blows on the front and back of his body, and in my experience those blows looked like ones you get if you were trying to protect someone against a much larger, stronger and tougher opponent. (Believe me, I know my stuff about that!)

It made sense in a way. I know Lord Gillman was a friend of the slaves and he always tried to help them, so he probably went to collect me an army, came back here for some reason and on the way he picked up a slave or two.

Then I know (or like to think) he would have tried to help them. Maybe he healed them, gave some food or just showed them a piece of kindness that the other Masters would never have given them.

Of course solving that mystery hardly helped me find Lord Gillman.

I knelt on the ground again when I could have sworn I'd heard the sound of breathing coming close by.

The sound got louder and louder. It sounded like someone was breathing heavily out of fear, not physical excursion.

It was coming from under the bed so I tapped on the bed frame and a door popped open.

Someone screamed. They crawled out and started running.

I tackled them. Covering their mouth with my hand.

Knowing this place I probably didn't need to make someone quiet because these disgraceful people would probably think I was having fun with someone, but I didn't want this person to be scared.

They kept struggling.

"Relax, I'm not a Master. I'm not a person who would use you. I am here to help you,"

Now the person had stopped struggling a little, I managed to see that this was a strong young woman with golden eyes, long gold hair and she was wearing nothing more than cheap cloth.

"What's your name?" I asked.

"Number 329," she said.

Wow. Of course, this place doesn't value people

enough to give them a name, only a number.

"What's his name?" I asked, pointing to the top of the bed.

"He was ma boyfriend Number 490,"

I didn't know if it was touching or strange that these slaves actually had relationships.

"I am here to help you. Can I get off you without you running away?"

"Yes Master," she said.

I didn't have time to argue with her that I wasn't a Master. I hated the term. I hated everything about this place, but it was probably just automatic for her to say that.

I got off her and helped her up. She looked so terrified as I helped her. It was probably confused by the offer and act of help.

"I am looking for Lord Gillman. Where is he?"

The woman looked at her boyfriend. "The Creature took him,"

"The Creature? Does the Creature work for the True Master?"

The woman didn't answer.

"Where would the Creature take my friend?" I asked.

The woman looked so confused by that question.

"You really aren't from here, are you?"

I smiled and shook my head.

"The Creature took your friend to the Shrine Of Pleasure at the very base of the Spires,"

I hugged her. "Thank you!"

I was about to leave when she grabbed my arm.

"Master Gillman instructed me to gather up Rebel Slaves. Is that still my Orders, Master?"

I just went along with her. "Yes,"

"Okay Master,"

It was heart-breaking telling a young woman these things.

I looked at her arm that was still grabbing mine and I gestured her to remove it.

She did but slowly.

"Um Master, the Creature isn't working for the True Master. The True Master is the Creature,"

CHAPTER 12
40 Hours Until the Rebellion Falls

Coleman felt his stomach churn as he looked over the edge of a small sandstone hill that allowed him to stare at the massive Catapults slowly moving below him.

If going through the underground temple, fighting more soldiers and having to evade the enemy long enough to get into position hadn't been bad enough, Coleman was getting more and more irritated by the massive brutes guarding and pushing the Catapults.

Unlike normal guards these Brutes wore bright red armour with budging muscles almost popping out of their armour, their arms, legs and chests were muscle factories, and their entire purpose seemed simple enough to Coleman. These brutes were born, bred and created for the sole purpose of killing and pushing Catapults around. It was hard from a perfect life, but Coleman had little doubt these people weren't intelligent enough to know what a good life was.

Especially as the only sound that came from these brutes were groans. Coleman doubted these people could just speak, bless them.

But just because they couldn't speak didn't mean they wouldn't kill Coleman, the two Archers and three Rebels that were left. Coleman had to be smart here or risk everything and the fate of the Kingdom.

Whooshing, cheering and shouting filled the air as the catapults fired again and Coleman forced down a hiss of pain as he saw the flaming rocks smash into more of the wall.

Considering he had been gone for hours trying to get here, Coleman was impressed that Richard had managed to ensure the Wall held together as even from this distance Coleman could see the Wall was failing. Especially with five catapults attacking it every few minutes.

Taking out his sword, Coleman was about to think of a plan, then the five remaining troops he had knelt down next to him.

"We can't fight 'em," someone said.

Coleman really wished Abbic was here. He needed someone he could trust by his side and Abbic was an amazing fighter so if things went south then at least there was a tiny chance they would make it back to the City.

"Bombo, got any knives on ya?" one of the Archers said to the other.

"Aye," Bombo said.

Coleman's eyes narrowed on the tall skinny man called Bombo with a massive ginger beard, grey hair and shaky hands. He was a bit surprised the Archer would fire straight.

"Coleman," Bombo said, passing him the knives.

Coleman's eyes widened as he realised what the Archers were hinting at. They clearly wanted him to throw the knives at the ropes that supported the Catapults. And the best thing was (at least to Coleman, not the enemy) that he didn't need to cut them completely, all he needed to do was damage the ropes enough so the strain of firing the next rock would destroy the ropes.

It was risky. Coleman hadn't practised throwing knives for years, decades even.

He held out the knives for someone else, but everyone smiled and shook their heads. Typical!

Coleman saw massive groups of brutes down below start to load up the catapults.

"Now or never," Coleman muttered to himself.

Coleman checked to see how many knives he had. He only had five shots to do as much damage as he could.

He raised the first knife. Aiming it at the catapult directly below him. Its main rope that attached the throwing arm to the frame was exposed enough.

Coleman threw it.

The knife chomped into the rope. Slicing it.

Coleman closed his eyes and listened for the

characteristic squeaking of the rope against the pressure of the throwing arm.

It was there.

Coleman took out the second knife. He aimed for another catapult a bit further out. The needed rope was a bit harder to see.

Coleman threw it.

The knife ripped into the rope. Slicing it cleanly. Then the knife dropped. Landing on a brute's head.

Coleman and the others ducked. But the brutes dismissed it.

Bombo came up to Coleman's ear to whisper.

"Coleman, aim for the catapult at the back. If you bring it down the others will be trapped,"

Coleman nodded. He focused on the back catapult but he could barely see the rope he needed to cut.

Coleman threw it.

The knife missed. Slamming into the throwing arm.

The brutes groaned.

Coleman threw again.

The fourth knife missed completely. It flew towards a brute. It slammed into a brute's eye.

The Brutes were alerted.

They pointed to Coleman.

Coleman threw the final knife.

It sliced through the rope.

The Catapults fired.

The rope screamed.

The wood screamed.

They smashed to the ground.

Creating a cloud of dust.

Coleman jumped up.

Everyone else did.

They ran back away.

Coleman wasn't going to fight thousands of men to destroy two catapults.

Cannons exploded.

People screamed inside the City.

Coleman kept running.

He knew the attack from the sea had begun.

Time was seriously running out now.

And Coleman didn't know what to do.

CHAPTER 13
40 Hours Until the Rebellion Falls

Damn it!

I am really, really starting to hate this True Master. Because of him I missed my deadline with the Hunters so no doubt I'm going to have to fight, struggle and hopefully survive an attack from them. I don't even know if that's possible.

I took out my swords and pulled my long black cloak and hood over me as I entered the so-called Shrine of Pleasure. Considering it had taken me hours to climb down here through the Spires, I was at least expecting something a bit grander.

The massive dirty stone arches lined an even larger (and horrible) circular chamber that I entered. The marble floor was covered in some strange symbols and the smell of blood, semen and sweat assaulted my senses.

I might not have been able to see the True Master or Lord Gillman but this was definitely the place where the True Master pleasured his victims.

The sound of strange groaning, moaning and hissing made me look up to see something that utterly horrified me. On the ceiling of the Shrine was a strange beastial looking creature with a long worm-like hairy body and eight limbs.

But these limbs weren't like arms, legs or claws. They were more akin to strange sex objects with the very tip of the limbs leaking something. This was beyond strange and I just wanted to leave.

No, actually I tell a lie. I wanted, needed to grab a flaming torch, throw it at the Creature and watch its corpse burn to ash. Then it would feel a lot safer. But what really disturbed me (out of the millions of things that this situation that did) was I couldn't see a head or a worm or insect equivalent.

A massive groan came from the Creature and I watched its limb move around and in the very centre of this monstrous sight was Lord Gillman. At least it looked like him. His entire body looked to be covered in a strange type of white silk that covered him completely.

Through the white silk I could just about see his face and it was a horrific mix of pure, utter pleasure and sheer terror. I wasn't sure if he wanted this or not. But judging by the hissing and moaning that I now understood was coming from him, I think it's fair to say he didn't want this.

Then the white silk started to turn red. Blood dripped onto the ground. The Creature was killing him.

I couldn't let Gillman die. I needed him.

"Stop!" I shouted.

I threw my swords at the Creature.

They sliced into its flesh.

Thick white blood poured out.

My swords fell. I rushed over. Picking them up.

The Creature shrieked.

Dropping Gillman's body.

I dashed. I was too late. His body slammed into the ground.

The Creature hissed.

It flew at me. It was quick. Dangerously quick.

It wrapped around Gillman's body.

One of its limbs whacked me.

Knocking me away.

I stood firm. Whipping out my swords. I charged.

I flew at the Creature.

Four limbs swung at me.

I jumped into the air.

Swirling and whirling.

I sliced through the limbs.

I ducked. Slicing through more.

The Creature hissed. It screamed. It moaned.

It thrusted a limb into Gillman. I could hear him screaming. Part in pleasure. Part in agony.

I charged over.

The Creature unleashed a supersonic shriek.

I collapsed to the ground. Covering my ears. My

vision blurred.

Gillman screamed.

Something whacked me across the Shrine.

Slamming me into a wall.

My vision cleared.

As my eyes fully adjusted to the Shrine once more, rage filled me as I stared at the bloodied dying body of Gillman. The Creature was gone, a small trail of white blood led away from the Shrine. But I didn't care at that moment.

I went over to the dying bloodied body of Gillman and just held him in my arms. He looked at me. As the life slowly drained from him, he had the decency to place his hands over his manhood where I knew there was a massive hole from the Creature's limbs.

Gillman didn't stare at me like I had failed him. Like I had failed to protect him, his people and my Rebellion. He looked at me as if he was the failure. I couldn't have him dying feeling like that.

"You did your best. You gave me hope. The first person in a long time," I said.

He smiled at that and as bright pink blood floated out of his mouth he tried to force out something. I couldn't understand it in the slightest, but there were three words that I did understand enough.

Smash my desk.

Of course I didn't know what that meant, why I needed to but considering I was now out of leads, my mission was as good as dead and my beautiful Coleman could be killed for my failure. I had to try.

Gillman grabbed me.

His eyes were glassy. His skin cold. Pink blood leaked from his eyes.

He smiled at me. It was a smile of a predator.

He pulled me closer.

His mouth opened. A massive worm-like limb poured out. Leaking something.

I shot back.

Whipping out my swords.

Ramming them in his throat.

As Gillman's body turned to ash I knew something was extremely wrong now. That Creature or True Master wasn't having sex for pleasure, it was reproducing, creating those monsters or slaves or whatever it called them.

I ran out of the Shrine knowing I had to save the City of Pleasure not only from the Overlord's control but something far, far darker.

CHAPTER 14
36 Hours Until the Rebellion Falls

Coleman whipped out his sword as he, the two Archers and three Rebels returned to the City of Martyrs to see it in utter chaos. Most of the little white houses were a raging inferno. The yellow cobblestone roads ran with blood.

Coleman led everyone through the City towards the main port where presumably the ships with cannons were attacking. Everyone kept their swords and bows aimed at corners of the streets, the doorways and roofs of the little white houses.

No one wanted to be caught off guard here.

Coleman couldn't believe this was happening. He had tried to plan for everything but two days was not going to be enough to plan for a sea invasion.

He had ordered countless ships to be wrecked to stop Overlord Battleships from entering the port but apparently that had been repeatedly vetoed by Richard's posh friends.

The idiots!

Now Coleman was really starting to understand why the Assassin hated politics, politicians and everything to do with them. They hardly ever did the right thing and at the end of the day, it was always down to people of action and more practical people to save the day.

Coleman had no idea where these posh friends were right now, but he knew they weren't fighting for their lives.

Two enemy soldiers ran at Coleman.

The Archers fired.

As Coleman nodded his thanks but the enemy was everywhere and the more Coleman focused on the corpses of the soldiers, the more he felt like something terrible was happening.

The soldier's uniforms weren't black like the Overlord's other soldiers, their uniform was dark, dark blue and Coleman felt as if he had seen these types of soldiers before. He had. Coleman didn't remember all the details but he remembered something about Naval elites.

Coleman sat at the corpses as he now had a very dangerous question to answer. In the rare case that the battleships weren't in the port, how did these enemy elites get into the City?

A cannon fired.

Little white houses shattered.,

Coleman jumped to one side.

A cannon flew past him.

He looked at the others. They nodded. Everyone ran towards the port.

The heat of the fires licked their flesh. The sounds of crackling fires were everywhere. The smell of black smoke infected every breath.

Coleman kept moving.

He had to get to the port.

When he reached the top of the hill, he stopped immediately. The long yellow cobblestone path down to the port wasn't yellow anyone. It was pure red as corpses of Rebels and soldiers like littered the path.

The smell of black toxic smoke was overwhelming but at the very bottom of the path at the port where a legion of tiny wooden boats docking, shouting and unloading hundreds of elites.

When each person got off their boat, they didn't wait to form a formation with their brothers and sisters in arms. They whipped out their swords and charged into the City.

Enemies were charging towards Coleman, the Archers and Rebels.

There were no reinforcements nearby. Coleman was alone.

He saw well over ten flashes as cannon balls were fired. All heading in his direction.

Coleman was ready to make a final stand.

CHAPTER 15

38 Hours Until the Rebellion Falls

Something was definitely happening outside on the streets of the City as I stormed into Gillman's office. All I could hear outside was people screaming in utter terror as something was shrieking.

It had to have something to do with the Creature and his reproducing. I wanted to go and check but something inside me was shouting at me to smash up Gillman's desk. If there was any hope for the City of Pleasure I was hoping, praying, demanding that there would be something inside the desk to help me.

I completely ignored the bloody corpse on the large golden bed and I went straight over to the small desk. I didn't look special or important but maybe that was what Gilman wanted. In my experience there's no better hiding spot for anything than in plain sight.

I opened the draws in the desk and hissed as my long black cloak got caught on a corner. The desk were filled with sexual objects, erotic drawings and packs of food. All great for him and the slaves but useless to me.

Taking out my swords I struck the desk repeatedly. Beating it into a wreckage of its former self.

When only large chunks of wood were left of the desk, I huffed as this was really started to annoy me now. So I kicked through the chunks of the wood and I sound something. It sounded like something metal hitting wood.

I knelt down on the ground and searched through the chunks and found something. It looked to be a small metal box. It was hardly that big, it was a lot smaller than a cash box but slightly bigger than the sort of box you get when you gift something expensive jewellery.

I grabbed a sword and popped it open.

There was nothing of great interest in the box, there was only a journal inside. I flipped through the journal and coughed as the sound of musty old paper filled my nose.

But when I actually started to read it, it was filled with journal entrances about the slaves, the ones they sent to the capital and something about baby Jasper.

A lump formed in my throat as I realised I was the baby Jasper. There were a few details I knew in the journal, including a rather passionate and rageful entry about hearing the Overlord throwing me and my brother in the river.

I tucked the journal safely away from in my long black cloak and prayed to the Gods and Goddesses that I got to read it all at some point. I had to have my answers.

I got up to leave when I noticed something off about the metal box itself. It seemed bigger on the outside than the inside. I mean the inside of the box should have been deeper than it actually was, not by much, maybe a few centimetres.

So I grabbed my swords and pounded the box until it cracked. Revealing two things, a long ivory dagger that was covered with white blood at the tip and a simple note.

I put the ivory dagger in my pocket along with the white shard I had from the mask of the Maiden of Light to use against the Hunters that I got a while ago.

When I read it, it couldn't really understand it at first but by the time I finished it, it was clearly about the Creature and what it was doing. It seemed there had only ever been one survivor (my mother) and she had described the experience, the powers and the wants of the Creature.

But it was the last part that really interested it.

The Day of Enlightenment shall come sooner than anyone ever thought. The City will embrace Master's pleasure and be longing for it. For He is divine and the pleasure is amazing, the only hope is the Ivory dagger to be forced through his mouth, just as I did.

Wow! I didn't know much about my mother but

she sounded like a bad-ass. But this was all too much, I didn't know how to handle all this information. Ten minutes ago, I had known nothing about her to almost knowing everything.

It was too much.

A deafening scream came from behind me.

I jumped up. Spun around. Throwing my sword at one of the Creature's Monsters.

"Thank you," someone said. And I hadn't noticed that the young strong woman from earlier with her long golden hair and golden eyes was there before now.

"You're welcome," I said simply enough. But there was something off about all this, why was the Creature attacking now?

"Master Gillman would have wanted you to have that?" she said.

"Do you have my army?" I asked, probably colder than I wanted.

"Yes Master, the slaves are coming here. But…"

I stepped forward. "What?"

"Master, the slaves are being swarmed, infected, turned,"

I held both my swords in my hands and sighed. "Come on, take me to them. We're going to save them, kill the Creature and then you will help me,"

"Yes Master. Anything Master," she said.

As we left the office, I subtly padded the journal and the ivory dagger in my pockets. I had no idea what I was walking into but I had to be ready. And I had to try to protect these slaves. I needed them to save my beautiful Coleman.

But this Creature would infect and turn people into mindless Monsters.

And that terrified me.

CHAPTER 16
35 Hours Until the Rebellion Falls

Coleman was going to gut each and every one of these foul elites that tried to attack his City, kill his people and threaten their freedom. It was bad enough they had been stupid enough to attack in the first place, but now they were swarming Coleman and his friends. He had had enough.

He was going to stop them no matter what!

The blood-red cobblestone path down to the port was a graveyard. Bodies covered every inch of the path. More and more cannons fired.

More little white houses shattered.

Fatigue flooded Coleman's body as he slashed the throat of another elite. They had all been fighting for an hour now. No help was coming.

Coleman had sent two of the Rebels away to get help. They hadn't returned. They were probably dead.

The dark blue armoured elites kept running up the path towards them.

The Archers fired.

Coleman slashed his sword.

Slicing into the enemy's throats.

More blood splashed onto the path.

Coleman kept cutting them down.

More cannons fired.

Coleman saw the cannon balls.

He jumped out the way.

The balls smashed into the cobblestone.

Shattering it.

Deadly shards flew at them.

Coleman heard a Rebel scream.

She bled out in seconds.

A shard sliced Coleman's forehead.

Coleman hissed.

Blood dripped down his face. Into his eyes.

Two enemies grabbed Coleman. Forcing him to the ground. They smashed their fists into him.

Coleman's vision blurred. His teeth chipped. His mouth bloody.

Explosions echoed throughout the City.

It wasn't cannon fire. It was the exploding of wood. The two elites let go of Coleman.

Coleman jumped up.

Smashing their heads together.

The elites fell.

Coleman stomped on their heads.

With no enemies nearby Coleman took long deep breathes of the smoke filled air and watched as one by one the massive wooden warships of the Overlord exploded, water flooded each ship and they all sunk rapidly.

The air moved behind Coleman.

He ducked.

A sword rushed past.

Coleman spun on the ground. Kicking the enemy. Knocking their legs out from under them.

Coleman leapt on top of them. Grabbing their head. Smashing it into the cobblestones.

Shouting filled the path.

Coleman looked down at the port.

More enemies were charging up to him.

Coleman whipped out his sword.

A crossbow bolt shot at his sword.

Causing it to fly out of Coleman's hands.

Coleman was unarmed.

The enemy jumped.

They were about to tackle Coleman.

Glass bottles flew through the air.

Smashing into the enemy.

The enemy exploded.

Coleman jumped back. Shielding his eyes.

Bright blue fire engulfed the enemy. Turning them into liquid.

As more and more glass bottles smashed into the enemy, Coleman picked up his sword and was surprised to see enemies running away from the City as quickly as they could.

Most of the so-called elites were even pushing their wooden boats back out. Coleman had no idea where they would go now their ships were sunk, but Coleman was never going to underestimate these foul soldiers again. Once this was over, Coleman would definitely send out people to hunt these elites down and kill them all.

But now Coleman had much larger problems to deal with.

"That okay for ya Bossie," a very familiar voice said.

Coleman felt his body fill with excitement and his stomach flipped with happiness at the sound of Abbic's common voice. Her voice might have been rough but he was so glad to see her.

He ran over to her and hugged her. Then he realised she was carrying plenty of glass bottles filled with toxic, deadly and just plain old explosive chemicals. So he made sure not to hug her too much.

But it was great to see her in her bright shiny armour again. She wasn't here to deliver her chemical concoctions to him, she was here to fight and that delighted Coleman.

Panic screams filled the air as Coleman and Abbic spun around to the Wall.

Everyone was running as quickly as they could away from it.

Coleman wanted to run over. He didn't.

A deafening boom echoed for miles around as the Wall shattered. Creating a thick deadly cloud of dust, ash and powdered sandstone.

Coleman felt cold sweat drip down his face as

now the ten thousand enemy soldiers outside the Wall could happily storm the City.

And kill every single person.

CHAPTER 17
34 Hours Until the Rebellion Falls

This was worse than anything I ever could have imagined.

After hours fighting through these horrible narrow streets and watching the Creature's monsters hack away at the little wooden slave houses and infecting everyone they could. I stood at the very edge of the City of Pleasure on the massive stone wall that circled the entire City.

My swords were drawn and all around me stood hundreds of brave men and women armed with whatever they could find (which wasn't more than kitchen knives and pots and pans) as we all watched the foul horde of thousands of infected Slaves march towards us.

I hated the sounds of their groaning, moaning and hissing but I had to defeat them, protect these brave men and women and hopefully gather some forces to save the man I loved.

I raised my swords and jumped off the wall.

I landed hard.

I swung my swords.

Slicing into enemy flesh.

White blood poured out. Splashing everywhere.

I didn't stop.

My swords swirled in the air. Slashing enemies.

Slicing their flesh. Slicing their throats. Slicing their heads off.

Their groans got louder. They attacked harder.

I kept swinging my swords.

Hacking off their hands.

Chopping off their arms.

Shattering their heads.

They still came.

The brave men and women fought too. They threw stones at the enemy.

The stones smashed into the enemy. Shattering bone. Splitting open heads.

I jumped into the air. Spinning around. Becoming a hurricane of death.

My swords chomping on all they touched.

The enemy hissed.

I kicked them. Breaking bones.

They were moving faster now. They kept coming. They focused on me.

I was being overwhelmed.

Screams came from above me.

I swung my sword in a bloody arc. I looked up.

The brave men and women were being attacked.

They were being infected.

I had to save them.

I kept swirling. I kept hacking the enemy apart. I had to get to them.

Hands grabbed me.

Pulling me to the ground.

I fell.

Warm liquid covered me.

I stared at the enemy. I struggled.

The enemy grabbed my arms. I couldn't swing my swords.

Their mouths opened. Something grew out of their throats.

They were coming towards me. Leaking something.

I screamed.

Something burnt in my pocket. White light shone out.

The enemy released me. Moving back. I whipped out the ivory dagger.

They hissed louder and louder.

I charged at them.

Slashing them with the dagger.

They turned to ash.

They screamed as loud as they could. They were calling something.

I had to silence them.

Something screamed back. They flew at me.

I swung the dagger wildly. Turning the infected to ash.

There were so many.

They whacked me against the outer wall.

I dropped the dagger.

They laughed.

They came to me.

Their mouths opened.

Then everyone stopped as we heard something stomp towards us. The silly infected people stepped to one side to create a path. My mouth dropped as I watched the massive Creature move towards me.

I didn't know how it was moving but as the sounds of cracking wood, falling buildings and screams filled my senses, I knew it was moving through the City and crushing whatever it wanted. I could see the hairy worm-like body of it and my stomach churned.

I didn't want to fight it. I didn't want to die.

I rushed over and grabbed the ivory dagger. The Infected slaves didn't seem to bat an eyelid. They truly didn't believe I could kill the Creature.

Three whooshes filled my senses.

The Hunters appeared in front of me.

They whipped out their swords.

I pointed behind them.

They hissed.

They ignored me. Their shadowy swords pointed at the Creature.

The Creature roared.

Charging towards us.

CHAPTER 18
34 Hours Until the Rebellion Falls

Coleman felt horrible sand, dust and ash coat his skin and throat as he marched up to the shattered Wall where ten thousand Overlord Soldiers were pouring into the City like an unstoppable tidal wave.

He grabbed a bow and arrows from a corpse.

Coleman aimed.

He fired.

An arrow flew through the air. Ramming itself in an enemy's brain.

More flew at him.

Coleman fired again.

And again.

Two more corpses dropped.

The enemy were getting too close.

Abbic ran over. Throwing her glass bottles.

Soldiers screamed as they melt. Their liquified flesh covered the cobblestones.

Coleman whipped out his sword. He had to find

Richard. He had to find survivors.

Coleman dived into the battle.

He swung his sword rapidly.

Chopping down the enemy.

Abbic covered him. She threw bottles.

More enemies burnt alive.

Coleman hacked through the soldiers.

Swords flashed past him.

Coleman ducked.

Abbic hissed.

Coleman heard shattering glass.

Abbic screamed.

Coleman slashed the soldier.

He spun around. Abbic was burning.

He grabbed her. Ripping off her armour.

Coleman threw the burning armour into the soldiers.

They screamed. They burnt. They died.

Coleman threw Abbic to the ground. She rolled around until the fire was out.

Someone whacked Coleman round the face.

They picked him up. Throwing him into the soldiers.

Swords sliced at him.

Coleman tried to jump up.

Soldiers stomped on him.

Coleman wrapped his arms around his head.

Magical energy crackled around him.

Lightning shot through the enemy.

Someone grabbed Coleman. Coleman jumped

up. Abbic pulled him away.

Richard stormed towards the soldiers. Magical energy scouring them.

Coleman raised his sword to join him. He went to charge over. Abbic grabbed him.

Whooshing filled the City. Tens of arrows screamed through the air.

Slamming into Richard. He dropped to the ground.

Coleman looked at Abbic. He had to save his friend. Abbic nodded.

Coleman ran towards Richard.

Abbic followed him. Throwing her bottles. The enemy slowed.

Coleman grabbed Richard. Pulling him away.

Richard tried to stand. He couldn't. Coleman kept pulling him.

Abbic stopped throwing bottles. She was out of them.

She grabbed Richard. Helping Coleman. This wasn't what Coleman needed.

Posh snobs ran past Coleman. He wanted to stop them.

The enemy open fired. Slaughtering the rich and powerful snobs.

Coleman kept pulling.

The rich snobs were buying him time.

And now Coleman knew that his entire fate rested in the hands of the Assassin.

She had to get here soon.

CHAPTER 19

34 Hours Until the Rebellion Falls

I flat out hated the Creature.

It charged at me and the Hunters. The Hunters disappeared. I dived out the way.

The Creature swung its limbs at me.

I jumped up.

Swinging my swords.

My swords sliced the limbs. No blood came out.

The Creature screamed.

They infected slaves charged.

The Hunters appeared.

Each one in front of a third of the infected.

Their shadowy swords sliced them.

Cutting them to pieces. They were stopping the infected from hurting me.

I flew at the Creature.

My swords swinging wildly.

The Creature's limbs met my swords.

The force making my hands ache.

Pain shot into my arms.

The Creature surged forward.

Knocking me back.

The Creature dived for me.

I threw a sword.

My sword slammed into its stomach.

It screamed.

I rolled. Jumping up. Whipping out the ivory dagger.

The Creature shrieked at the sight.

I ran at it.

Jumping into the air.

The Creature's limbs flew at me.

Wrapping around my waist.

Wrapping my head.

Wrapping around my wrists.

They squeezed.

I dropped the ivory dagger. The limb around my head stopped. It grabbed the ivory dagger.

Crushing it. The dagger shattered. My heart dropped.

Rage filled me.

I swung my sword. It sliced the Creature.

The limbs released me. I fell to the ground. I landed hard. My knees ached.

The Creature whacked me against the wall.

The back of my head cracked against the wall. My sight went black.

I couched at the ground with my world completely black except for the odd slivers of light at the very corners of my vision.

I was expecting the Creature to just finish me off but I heard it turn and started attacking. He was presumably attacking the Hunters.

The Hunters deserved to die for what they tried to do to me. But they were innocent. They were trapped by a magic bond of some sort. I had to save them.

Something wet slammed me against the outer wall. I felt something growing over my skin. It felt great. Wonderful. It felt pleasurable.

No!

I wasn't letting the Creature do something to me. A wave of strange energy dripped into my blood as more and more of my skin started to tinkle.

This had to be the Creature pouring his corruption into me but the energy felt as if it was coming from my cells and within me. It wasn't coming from the stuff on my skin.

Then it twigged. My mother was the only survivor of the Creature. She apparently had strange magical powers. Maybe I inherited them!

More and more energy filled me and my sight started to return. I was covered in fine white silk and I felt myself smiling.

I stopped that. I was not smiling. I was not happy. I was fuming!

Magical energy surged inside me.

I thrusted out my hands. Shattering the white silk and limb like it was nothing.

It was nothing. I hated this Creature.

The Creature shot back at the sight of me.

Even the Hunters disappeared.

White magical energy shone out of me.

The Creature froze. I didn't.

I charged forward.

My swords flew over to me.

I raised them.

Jumping into the air.

The Creature swung its limbs at me.

I sliced them.

The limbs turned to crystal.

They shattered.

The Creature tried to run.

It couldn't move.

I bought down my swords.

Magic energy shot out of them.

Turning the Creature to crystal.

I punched it and the entire Creature shattered. Turning to dust.

I blinked a couple of times as I felt the strange magical energy absorb back into my cells and I had no idea what had just happened. All I knew was that it had something to do with my mother.

People muttered to themselves and I realised that everyone who was still alive was no longer infected and they all stared at me with that annoying as hell human curiosity.

Someone clicked their fingers at me (the nerve!) and I looked up at the outer wall to see the strong young woman with her golden hair and eyes stared at me.

Then she bowed.

Everyone bowed at me. I didn't want their praise. I wanted them to help me, help free my people, help me save the man I loved.

But as I looked around at their City, I realised it was all destroyed. These people had nothing left, not that they had a lot in the beginning. They were sex slaves.

Well, they *were* sex slaves. They were people now. People free to do as they pleased.

"Rise," I said.

Everyone looked at each other and then they rose with massive smiles on their faces. But all the previously infected people started coughing out of ash as presumably the thing inside their throats was now dead.

As dead as beautiful Coleman if I didn't hurry.

So I did something that I swore never to do. I knelt on the ground like all these people were superior to me. Because in that moment they were.

"You're welcome to your freedom. But I beg you, I truly beg you to help me. Come with me to the City of Martyrs and please, please help me save my friends,"

"Assassin!" the young strong woman shouted gesturing me to look at something.

I climbed up to the outer wall and looked over the area and my mouth dropped as maybe tens of thousands of different people from all different Cities, regions and every single part of the Kingdom rode past the City as fast as they could.

Coleman's message had inspired people to risk their lives.

"We Stand With the Rebellion," the young strong woman said.

I smiled. Maybe I could save the man I loved after all.

CHAPTER 20
0 Hours Until The Rebellion Falls

Coleman hated his idea of the Rebellion having over 30 hours to live. That was never going to happen. The Rebellion's time had ran out and he hated himself for it. How could he have been so arrogant to think they could have defended themselves. The Overlord was always going to win. That was the simple truth.

A massive thud echoed around the little house Coleman, Abbic and Richard were hiding in. The room was disgusting with its tiny size, layers of mould and pathetic door.

But it was all Coleman had time to find. Him and Abbic had tried to board up and reinforce the door as best they could and finally their building skills could be tested.

Another thud cracked the door and Coleman could see the soldiers outside with their battering ram.

Coleman looked at Abbic who was staring at the

door and like Coleman, she had cold fearful sweat dripping down her forehead. Coleman hated all of this, he wanted to do something.

He didn't know how many of his friends lived, how many of them were fighting or even how many of them hadn't been captured. Coleman just wanted to know they were okay.

He would happily give up his life for theirs. His friends never deserved to die.

Richard groaned a little as magic energy crackled around his wounds as he presumably tried to heal himself. Coleman wished he could help but medicine was never his specialist subject.

A final thud shattered the door.

Wooden shards flew towards them.

Coleman dived over Abbic and Richard.

Shards rammed themselves in his back.

Coleman hissed.

The soldiers poured out.

Ripping him away from Abbic and Coleman.

Another soldier kicked Richard in-between the legs.

Coleman felt a cold blade touch his throat.

Two other soldiers grabbed Richard and Abbic.

"See Commander Coleman. Watch your friends die," a man said.

The other soldiers with Abbic and Richard whipped out knives and raised them.

Coleman had to do something. He wouldn't let them die. His Assassin might have failed him. She wasn't coming. Coleman couldn't fail these two.

"Stop! I know something," Coleman shouted.

"I don't believe you. Kill them," the man said.

"If you kill them I will never tell you the secret,"

The man laughed. "Just do it,"

The two soldiers pressed the knives against Abbic's and Richard's throats. Coleman couldn't bear it. Blood dripped down their bodies.

Richard blinked at Coleman in a beat. He didn't know what it meant.

Coleman needed to half-act. "No. Please don't! Take me. Kill me please! Let them go!"

The man laughed again right in Coleman's ear as he gestured the soldiers to slowly kill them.

Richard smiled. He shot out his hands. Magical lightning shot out. Killing the soldiers.

Coleman grabbed the man's sword.

More soldiers poured in.

Coleman slashed their chests.

Abbic grabbed two more swords. She attacked. Hacking the enemy to pieces.

A deafening sound echoed throughout the City. Coleman didn't know what it was but it made all the soldiers run away from them and towards the Wall.

Coleman went out of the little white house they were in and looked at what the soldiers were so scared. And utter delight filled him as he saw in far, far distance tens of thousands (probably hundreds of thousands in reality) of people were riding towards them.

And there was a little black dot at the very front of the mass of people. A little black dot with a long black cloak and hood flapping in the wind.

Coleman's stunning sexy Assassin had come for him at last.

CHAPTER 21
0 Hours Until Rebellion Falls

I was finally going to save the man I loved. The man I needed to protect, treasure and made sure he survived. Not only for me but to ensure the freedom of the entire Kingdom, and that was why tens of thousands of amazing people rode behind me.

I kicked my horse to ride faster.

My horse went faster and faster and faster. We had to reach the City of Martyrs. I could see the thousands of foul enemies in the City. They weren't claiming my beautiful Coleman today, or any other day for that matter.

I was leading the mass of riders towards the City. I just wished they would hurry up and help me storm the City but the wind was awful so I couldn't blame them too much. My long black cloak and hood was flapping about wildly.

The Hunters appeared in front of me. They flicked out their hands.

Throwing me off my horse. My horse kept riding.

I jumped up. Staring at the Hunter's black cloaks and shadowy faces. They whipped out their shadowy swords.

I whipped out my swords. The Shadows flew at me.

Our swords clashed.

Magical energy crackled around us.

I jumped into the air. Swirling around. My blade whirling.

The Hunters' swung. Knocking me to the ground.

My back pounded the ground.

The Hunters grabbed me. I screamed. Their icy touch burning me.

I struggled. I kicked. I punched.

More icy pain flooded my senses.

In the back of my mind I heard Coleman's voice. He needed me. I had to protect them.

I screamed through the pain. I leapt up. Swinging my swords in a bloody arc.

The Hunters shot back.

Raising their hands.

Black energy shot out.

It slammed into me. Burning my cloak.

I sank to my knees in agony.

I heard horses thunder towards us. Tens of thousands of people were close. I felt the hooves pound behind me.

The pain lessened. Hunters were distracted.

I dived forward.

Whipping out the white shard. The Hunters screamed at the sight. The shard shone bright light.

A ghostly form of the Maiden of Light appeared.

The Hunters screamed in terror.

I jumped forward.

Slicing a Hunter with the shard.

It shrieked.

They all disappeared.

But when I looked back at the white shard from the mask of the Maiden of Light (the woman who birthed them), all I saw was ash in my hands. I might have saved myself this time but now I didn't have a weapon to use against them.

My only hope now was to find that oath rode if such a thing even existed, and then I just had to hope beyond hope that the Hunters wouldn't kill me after I freed them.

With the sound of tens of thousands of amazing men and women thundering behind me, I whistled for my horse and hopped on.

Riding towards the City of Martyrs to save, protect and treasure the man I loved.

I just hoped he was still alive.

CHAPTER 22
1 Hour After Rebellion Was Saved

Commander Coleman felt immense waves of happiness, delight and affection wash over him as he stared at all the wonderful people around him.

In amongst the wreckage, the burning little white houses and corpses stood tens of thousands of people that had dared to do the unthinkable. They had all left their comfortable homes and Cities and rode for Gods know how long all to come to his aid.

A man denounced by the Overlord as a crazy, traitor that wanted everyone in the Kingdom to die. But all these people had come.

Coleman had never seen so many people from so many different classes, regions and Cities. He didn't recognise half the accents, the dialects and even some of the food these people had bought for him and his friends.

He might have not have known these people, leaders or their interest in the Rebellion, but as

Coleman breathed in the wonderful sweet fruit smells of the mini-desserts of these people. It was clear these people wanted him to do well.

Later he would have to talk seriously to each of the leaders so he could understand what was happening better, but for now, he just wanted a little moment of peace. After all him, Abbic and all the other survivors had just survived a massacre.

All because of his girlfriend the Assassin with her stunning dark eyes, long black cloak and hood and her wonderful smile that would always melt his heart.

When this mass of people stormed the City and immediately started killing the Overlord's soldiers, Coleman had tried to look for the Assassin but he couldn't find her. He knew she was alive, he would have liked to think if anything had happened to her he would feel it in his bones.

People cheered, shouted and laughed as they picked through the wreckage, and there was something so warming about it.

After days of fighting, bloodshed and sadness, it was amazing (to Coleman at least) to see people who had never met before laughing and bonding over mocking the Overlord. A few metres from Coleman was a man with dark skin laughing with another man as he gave him some of the corpse's armour.

Coleman didn't know what they were laughing about, but they weren't the only ones. Even in this strange time after a massive loss and a victory, everyone was finding the joy in it.

Maybe they were happy that the Overlord could be defeated.

And that reminded Coleman of one of his worse fears that was thankfully proved wrong. At the start of the slaughter, Coleman had been terrified that if he lost it would send a message throughout the Kingdom telling everyone how the Overlord could never ever be defeated.

As Coleman looked around with a massive smile on his face, he knew the Overlord had been proved very wrong. He was even more impressed when Lord Castellan Richard had sent out ten messengers sending in every direction in the Kingdom to tell others about the Overlord's defeat.

That was bold.

Yet it was needed. The people of the Kingdom needed to know the power of the people and the Rebellion when they helped each other anything was possible.

Coleman might not have known what the future held but he was looking forward to it. He looked forward to storming the capital, killing the Overlord and freeing the people of the Kingdom.

As he walked off into the crowd, he realised the storming of the capital was definitely something for thinking about tomorrow, today he wanted to talk to the other leaders then see the most important person in the entire City.

Coleman was going to have a long overdue catch-up (and hopefully more) with his beautiful

Assassin.
Finally.

CHAPTER 23
Two Hours After Rebellion Was Saved

After a couple of good hours, I had finally found a person who was willing to make me a good cup of coffee without any of that horrible almond syrup. That was probably the highlight of my day!

With most of the City burning, destroyed or just no longer standing, I sat on one of the few remaining granite towers of the Wall with my legs dangling over the edge with a wonderful view of the City below me.

Of course the idea of sitting on the edge of a building that could collapse was scary to most people, but after the past few days I just wanted a quiet place to sit and get a precious few moments of silence before something else happened.

I loved the amazing warm feeling of the mug of coffee in my hands and I loved the bitter smell of the coffee even more. It was a great contrast to the foul smells of the past few days.

But I will mention one thing I am surprised about. Normally when Coleman sends out a note, a message or anything, no one cares. No one cares about the Rebellion, no one wants to help them out because of fear of the Overlord burning their family to ash. And yet this time they came.

When I was riding here with the City of Pleasure and the other tens of thousands of people, I actually asked them why did they come. Their answer surprised me. It was all because of me.

Apparently news of my skills, hatred for the Overlord and actions had reached every corner of the Kingdom and it inspired people. Then apparently because I believed in Coleman, people trusted my judgement so they followed him.

I'm not really sure how to take that really. I have never seen myself as a great warrior, an inspirational person or even that good at all that moral character stuff. I'm just an assassin who got caught up in the Rebellion's great cause.

Damn them!

The laughter, talking and shouting of tens of thousands below me was such a strange sound after everything. People were happy here and in all honesty I could understand it. I really could. For them there was a chance of happiness and freedom, a real chance for the first time in fifty years.

Forgetting about the battle and fighting for each City for a moment, I picked the journal and opened it on the very last page. It turned out Lord Gillman didn't fail me or himself anything.

There was a map on the very last page but I couldn't understand it. It was made up of so many crazy lines and symbols and words in another language. I would have to scout out the City of Martyrs tomorrow to find someone who could understand all this.

But the journal. It made for interesting reading and now I sort of felt like I didn't know myself anymore. Turned out my mother was a simple farm girl who was captured, shipped and trained in the City of Pleasure decades ago. She rose through their ranks and became the most popular slave in the entire City.

The Masters treated her well and the other slaves were so jealous they tried to kill her on at least ten occasions over the decades. Then the True Master selected her for a pleasure session and that's when everything changed apparently.

Whilst Lord Gillman might have been her only true friend in the City, he didn't have a gift for describing what had happened next. All I could gather from his writings were my mother fought back using the ivory dagger, resisted its corrupting influence and become changed somewhat.

Now I don't know what my mother was truly like but Gillman made it sound like she become a sort of Seer. Able to see the future, perform most types of limited magic and something about her being a holy figure except when she was with him.

I have no idea how I feel about that personally, it seems so strange and made-up but I don't know how to explain my own magic during that battle. It had to come from my mother.

I really don't know what to think about at this time.

Then the Overlord came, collected her and that was the end of the writings really. After that it was simply Gillman journaling and channelling his rage at what the Overlord had done to my mother, me and my brother.

My beautiful precious brother, the Overlord will pay for killing him.

I felt someone wrap their strong amazing arms around me and I was pulled towards someone. Coleman kissed me on the head and I stared into those wonderful dark emerald eyes.

Then I realised none of this stuff about my mother, the Overlord or the Rebellion mattered, at least not for a few hours.

I rolled over, pushed Coleman on the ground and I smiled.

With everything right with the world and everyone safe once again, I wasn't going to be an Assassin for a few hours. I was just going to be a woman with her boyfriend and I was going to enjoy it. A lot.

And that was fine by me.

After saving the Rebellion, the City of Pleasure and the Kingdom, I think I deserved a bit of pleasure myself.

And I was going to savour it.

AUTHOR'S NOTE

Thank you for reading, I really hope you enjoyed it.

In the Author's Note, I always like to mention quickly what inspired the book, and the main inspiration for this book was a very strange picture I saw once.

I think I must have been watching a history programme and they were talking about Pleasure Gardens in England during the 18th Century, so I was interested in that because I had never heard of Pleasure Gardens before.

Therefore, I started watching it and it turned out that one of the functions of Pleasure Gardens were brothels and as I was starting to write the City of Assassins short stories that got me thinking.

Then the programme showed an image of the Pleasure Gardens with tons of young women dressed in scandalously short stuff with their arms and ankles showing skin, (at least back then it was scandal) and they were all cramped together.

As well as you also have the fact that Coleman mentioned that he came from the City of Pleasure so it was worth exploring for that alone. Then the idea of the Masters, True Masters and monsters came from different places of course.

But in the first and last chapters, I mentioned the Assassin didn't like almond syrup in her coffee. Now I did this because at the time of writing, I got a range of flavoured coffee syrups for Christmas and there was a syrup I really didn't like.

It turns out it was actually an apricot syrup but I thought it was an almond so hence the dislike from the Assassin.

Overall, I really hope you enjoyed the book and see check out the rest of the series in electronic and print format at your favourite bookstore.

I hope to see you in another book soon.

Have a great day!

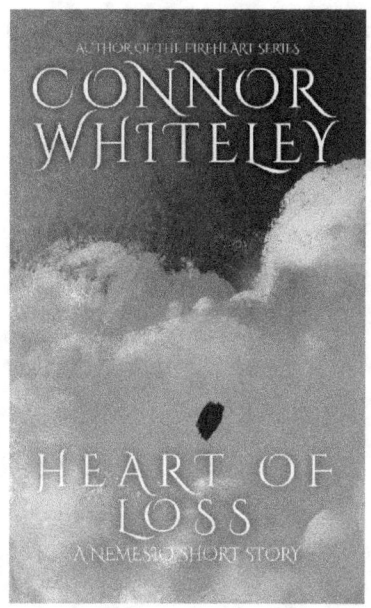

GET YOUR FREE AND EXCLUSIVE SHORT STORY NOW! LEARN ABOUT NEMESIO'S PAST!

https://www.subscribepage.com/fireheart

Keep up to date with exclusive deals on Connor Whiteley's Books, as well as the latest news about new releases and so much more!

Sign up for the Grab a Book and Chill Monthly newsletter, and you'll get one **FREE** ebook just for signing up: Agents of The Emperor Collection.

Sign Up Now!

https://dl.bookfunnel.com/f4p5xkprbk

About the author:

Connor Whiteley is the author of over 60 books in the sci-fi fantasy, nonfiction psychology and books for writer's genre and he is a Human Branding Speaker and Consultant.

He is a passionate Warhammer 40,000 reader, psychology student and author.

Who narrates his own audiobooks and he hosts The Psychology World Podcast.

All whilst studying Psychology at the University of Kent, England.

Also, he was a former Explorer Scout where he gave a speech to the Maltese President in August 2018 and he attended Prince Charles' 70th Birthday Party at Buckingham Palace in May 2018.

Plus, he is a self-confessed coffee lover!

OTHER SHORT STORIES BY CONNOR WHITELEY

Blade of The Emperor

Arbiter's Truth

The Bloodied Rose

Asmodia's Wrath

Heart of A Killer

Emissary of Blood

Computation of Battle

Old One's Wrath

Puppets and Masters

Ship of Plague

Interrogation

Edge of Failure

One Way Choice

Acceptable Losses

Balance of Power

Good Idea At The Time

Escape Plan

Escape In The Hesitation

Inspiration In Need

Singing Warriors

Dragon Coins

Dragon Tea

Dragon Rider

Knowledge is Power

Killer of Polluters

Climate of Death
Sacrifice of the Soul
Heart of The Flesheater
Heart of The Regent
Heart of The Standing
Feline of The Lost
Heart of The Story
The Family Mailing Affair
Defining Criminality
The Martian Affair
A Cheating Affair
The Little Café Affair
Mountain of Death
Prisoner's Fight
Claws of Death
Bitter Air
Honey Hunt
Blade On A Train
City of Fire
Awaiting Death
Poison In The Candy Cane
Christmas Innocence
You Better Watch Out
Christmas Theft
Trouble In Christmas
Smell of The Lake
Problem In A Car

Theft, Past and Team
Embezzler In The Room
A Strange Way To Go
A Horrible Way To Go
Ann Awful Way To Go
An Old Way To Go
A Fishy Way To Go
A Pointy Way To Go
A High Way To Go
A Fiery Way To Go
A Glassy Way To Go
A Chocolatey Way To Go
Kendra Detective Mystery Collection Volume 1
Kendra Detective Mystery Collection Volume 2
Stealing A Chance At Freedom
Glassblowing and Death
Theft of Independence
Cookie Thief
Marble Thief
Book Thief
Art Thief

Other books by Connor Whiteley:

The Fireheart Fantasy Series
Heart of Fire
Heart of Lies
Heart of Prophecy
Heart of Bones
Heart of Fate

City of Assassins (Urban Fantasy)
City of Death
City of Martyrs
City of Pleasure
City of Power

Agents of The Emperor
Return of The Ancient Ones
Vigilance
Angels of Fire

The Garro Series- Fantasy/Sci-fi
GARRO: GALAXY'S END
GARRO: RISE OF THE ORDER
GARRO: END TIMES
GARRO: SHORT STORIES
GARRO: COLLECTION
GARRO: HERESY

GARRO: FAITHLESS
GARRO: DESTROYER OF WORLDS
GARRO: COLLECTIONS BOOK 4-6
GARRO: MISTRESS OF BLOOD
GARRO: BEACON OF HOPE
GARRO: END OF DAYS

Winter Series- Fantasy Trilogy Books
WINTER'S COMING
WINTER'S HUNT
WINTER'S REVENGE
WINTER'S DISSENSION

Miscellaneous:
RETURN
FREEDOM
SALVATION
Reflection of Mount Flame
The Masked One
The Great Deer

All books in 'An Introductory Series':
BIOLOGICAL PSYCHOLOGY 3RD EDITION
COGNITIVE PSYCHOLOGY THIRD EDITION
SOCIAL PSYCHOLOGY- 3RD EDITION
ABNORMAL PSYCHOLOGY 3RD EDITION
PSYCHOLOGY OF RELATIONSHIPS- 3RD EDITION
DEVELOPMENTAL PSYCHOLOGY 3RD EDITION
HEALTH PSYCHOLOGY
RESEARCH IN PSYCHOLOGY
A GUIDE TO MENTAL HEALTH AND TREATMENT AROUND THE WORLD- A GLOBAL LOOK AT DEPRESSION
FORENSIC PSYCHOLOGY
THE FORENSIC PSYCHOLOGY OF THEFT, BURGLARY AND OTHER CRIMES AGAINST PROPERTY
CRIMINAL PROFILING: A FORENSIC PSYCHOLOGY GUIDE TO FBI PROFILING AND GEOGRAPHICAL AND STATISTICAL PROFILING.
CLINICAL PSYCHOLOGY
FORMULATION IN PSYCHOTHERAPY

PERSONALITY PSYCHOLOGY AND INDIVIDUAL DIFFERENCES
CLINICAL PSYCHOLOGY REFLECTIONS VOLUME 1
CLINICAL PSYCHOLOGY REFLECTIONS VOLUME 2
CULT PSYCHOLOGY
Police Psychology

Companion guides:
BIOLOGICAL PSYCHOLOGY 2ND EDITION WORKBOOK
COGNITIVE PSYCHOLOGY 2ND EDITION WORKBOOK
SOCIOCULTURAL PSYCHOLOGY 2ND EDITION WORKBOOK
ABNORMAL PSYCHOLOGY 2ND EDITION WORKBOOK
PSYCHOLOGY OF HUMAN RELATIONSHIPS 2ND EDITION WORKBOOK
HEALTH PSYCHOLOGY WORKBOOK
FORENSIC PSYCHOLOGY WORKBOOK

Audiobooks by Connor Whiteley:
BIOLOGICAL PSYCHOLOGY
COGNITIVE PSYCHOLOGY
SOCIOCULTURAL PSYCHOLOGY
ABNORMAL PSYCHOLOGY
PSYCHOLOGY OF HUMAN RELATIONSHIPS
HEALTH PSYCHOLOGY
DEVELOPMENTAL PSYCHOLOGY
RESEARCH IN PSYCHOLOGY
FORENSIC PSYCHOLOGY
GARRO: GALAXY'S END
GARRO: RISE OF THE ORDER
GARRO: SHORT STORIES
GARRO: END TIMES
GARRO: COLLECTION
GARRO: HERESY
GARRO: FAITHLESS
GARRO: DESTROYER OF WORLDS
GARRO: COLLECTION BOOKS 4-6
GARRO: COLLECTION BOOKS 1-6

Business books:

TIME MANAGEMENT: A GUIDE FOR STUDENTS AND WORKERS

LEADERSHIP: WHAT MAKES A GOOD LEADER? A GUIDE FOR STUDENTS AND WORKERS.

BUSINESS SKILLS: HOW TO SURVIVE THE BUSINESS WORLD? A GUIDE FOR STUDENTS, EMPLOYEES AND EMPLOYERS.

BUSINESS COLLECTION

GET YOUR FREE BOOK AT:
WWW.CONNORWHITELEY.NET

www.ingramcontent.com/pod-product-compliance
Lightning Source LLC
LaVergne TN
LVHW012110070526
838202LV00056B/5688